A Special Kind of Love

Stephen Michael King

SCHOLASTIC PRESS / New York

For Trish
and Peter

Cataloging-in-Publication Data available
Library of Congress number: 95-21828

ISBN 0-590-67681-4

10 9 8 7 6 5 4 3

Printed in Singapore

First printing, May 1996

The illustrator used watercolors, black ink,
and colored pencils for the paintings in this book.

There once was a man

who had a son.

The son loved the man,

and the man loved boxes.

Big boxes.

Round boxes.

Small boxes.

Tall boxes.

All kinds of boxes!

The man loved his son, too,
but he had trouble telling him.

So with his boxes, the man began to make wonderful things for his son.

He was great at making castles,

and his planes would fly forever,

unless, of course,
it rained.

Boxes would suddenly appear
when friends came to stay.
And in those boxes
they would play . . .

and play . . .

and play.

Most people thought the man was very strange.

Old men
pointed at him.

Old ladies scowled at him.

Even his neighbors laughed at him behind his back.

But that never bothered the man,